BIKE & TRIKE

FOR SYLVIE, BRIAN B., MARY C., AND LUCY C.,
FOR TAKING THIS RIDE WITH ME—E. V.

FOR HANNAH AND STELLA—B. B.

SIMON & SCHUSTER BOOKS FOR YOUNG READERS

An imprint of Simon & Schuster Children's Publishing Division

1230 Avenue of the Americas, New York, New York 10020

SIMON & SCHUSTER BOOKS FOR YOUNG READERS is a trademark of Simon & Schuster, Inc.

For information about special discounts for bulk purchases, please contact

Simon & Schuster Special Sales at 1-866-506-1949 or business@simonandschuster.com.

The Simon & Schuster Speakers Bureau can bring authors to your live event. For more information or to book an event, contact

the Simon & Schuster Speakers Bureau at 1-866-248-3049 or visit our website at www.simonspeakers.com.

Also available in a Simon & Schuster Books for Young Readers hardcover edition

Book design by Lucy Ruth Cummins

The text for this book was set in Century Schoolbook.

The illustrations for this book were rendered in pencil and pixels.

Manufactured in China

0520 SCP

First Simon & Schuster Books for Young Readers paperback edition August 2020

2 4 6 8 10 9 7 5 3 1

The Library of Congress has cataloged the hardcover edition as follows:

Names: Verdick, Elizabeth, author. | Biggs, Brian, illustrator.

Title: Bike & Trike / Elizabeth Verdick ; illustrated by Brian Biggs.

Other titles: Bike and Trike

Description: First edition. | New York : Simon & Schuster Books for Young Readers, [2020] | "A Paula Wiseman Book." |

Summary: When Lulu graduates to a bicycle with training wheels, rusty,

old Trike feels lonely in the garage and worries about Lulu's safety on her shiny, new bike.

Identifiers: LCCN 2019006397| ISBN 9781534415171 (hardcover) | ISBN 9781534480438 (pbk) | ISBN 9781534415188 (eBook)

Subjects: | CYAC: Bicycles and bicycling—Fiction. | Growth—Fiction. | Friendship—Fiction.

Classification: LCC PZ7.1.V4615 Bi 2020 | DDC [E]—dc23

LC record available at https://lccn.loc.gov/2019006397

BIKE&TRIKE

ELIZABETH VERDICK & BRIAN BIGGS

A PAULA WISEMAN BOOK

Simon & Schuster Books for Young Readers

New York   London   Toronto   Sydney   New Delhi

Trike is a rusty little fellow,
a trusty little fellow,
on three worn-down wheels.

He sits parked in the dusty dark.
"Now that Lulu has outgrown me,"
he says, "I sure am lonely."

Through the years, he and Lulu had braved . . .

summer bees,

skinned knees,

a wet seat,

the big street . . .

and the time when
tiny Tru said,
"Uh-oh. No go."

One day, the garage door opens: *Grummmmm*.

In rolls a happy young fellow, a snappy
young fellow, on four spiffed-up wheels.

"Hi, I'm Bike!" says the new guy, his streamers waving.

"Oh, I'm Trike." Trike thinks of his own scratches and patches.

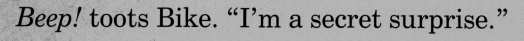

Beep! toots Bike. "I'm a secret surprise."

Lulu's birthday, thinks Trike.

Bike is . . . for her.

Bike blasts past. "It's my—*whoa*—

first time—*whoops*—out of the store."

"Look out!" says Trike.

Bike pops a wheelie: *wha-THUMP*.

"Bike," says Trike, "soon you'll meet your rider. Lulu is the nicest—"

"Watch *this* trick," says Bike, riding
through Hula Hoop. *Zazooma-zoom!*
"Safety first," says Trike.
"*Aw*, back off, old-timer," says Bike.
"I've got a need
for speed."

"It's crowded in here," says Bike.

"Let's open the door."

Ball pushes the button: *Bounce!*

Grummmmm goes the door.

Bike rolls outside. "That path looks fun.

Let's race, Trike."

Alone? thinks Trike. *Without riders?*

"First one to the woods is the
Winner on Wheels!" says Bike.

Hmmm. Trike knows each turn
and twist in that path.
Bike *doesn't*.

"I'll be the champ!" yells Bike.

"If *I* win," says Trike, "you have to *promise* to let Lulu ride at her own pace."

Bike nods. "*Okey-dokey*, poky."

Jump Rope forms the starting line.

The Pom-Poms cheer.

Whistle blows:

Pedal, pedal, pedal:

Trike's wheels squeak;

his metal parts creak.

Bike blows by:

PEDAL, PEDAL,

PEDAL, PEDAL!

Trike pushes harder.

Pedal-pedal-pedal.

"You can DO this," Trike tells himself,

"for *Lulu* and the way the two of us flew."

Trike . . . catches . . . up . . . to Bike.

From his handlebars to his wheels, Trike

feels a *ping* and a *zing-zing*.

His bell *ring-ring-rings* . . . the way it did

when Lulu was in the driver's seat.

Oops—

Trike's and Bike's back wheels go *bump*.

"OUCH!"

Bike shouts.

Trike stops to help. "Are you okay, Bike?"

Bike suddenly takes off—the *wrong* way.

"I'm going
FOUR-wheeling!"
calls Bike as
he heads off-road.

"A shortcut!"

Dip, dash—Bike's gone in a flash.

"The *cliff*!"
Trike gasps.

Bike doesn't know
how *steep* it is.

Trike *has* to head Bike off at the pass!

Trike *zip-zip-zips*, calling,

"*Biiiiike,*
HIT THE BRAKES!"

The grass is slick—

Trike loses his grip—

he *tip-tip-tips* . . .

"*That* was close—just missed the cliff!" says Trike.

"I guess we *both* went too fast, huh?"

"Yes," says Bike.

"I'm sorry for showing off.
I guess I have a
lot to learn."

"I can teach you,"
says Trike.

Bike leans over, streamers dangling. "Here, take my handlebar, Trike. I'll help you up."

Trike chuckles. "At least *one* part of me is new."

"Which part?" asks Bike.

"This *dent*."

Bike says, "I like you, Trike."

"Thanks, friend."

Bike and Trike ride side by side,
one big, one small—

two winners on wheels.

The next day—

a *birth*day—

Lulu and Tru . . .

hop on . . .

Beepa-beep!

Ring-ding!

and off they go!